GRACE STREET KIDS

MARTY &
THE MYSTERY GIFT

GRACE STREET KIDS

MARTY & THE MYSTERY GIFT

STANDARD
PUBLISHING

Marti Plemons

Grace Street Kids
Megan & the Owl Tree
Josh & the Guinea Pig
Georgie & the New Kid
Scott & the Ogre
Erin & the Special Promise
Michael & the Dark Cross
Marty & the Mystery Gift
Brooke & the Guilty Secret

Acquisition and editing by March Media, Inc.

The Standard Publishing Company, Cincinnati, Ohio
A division of Standex International Corporation

99 98 97 96 95 94 93 92   5 4 3 2 1

Library of Congress Cataloging-in-Publication Data

Plemons, Marti.
   Marty & the mystery gift / Marti Plemons.
     p. cm. — (Grace Street kids)
   Summary: Eleven-year-old Marty worries that she is the only kid on Grace Street
without some special talent, until she discovers that her spiritual gift need not be
creative and will manifest itself in God's own time.
   ISBN 0-87403-937-1
   [1. Christian life — Fiction. 2. Self-perception — Fiction.] I. Title. II. Title: Marty
and the mystery gift. III. Series: Plemons, Marti. Grace Street kids.
PZ7.P718Mar 1992
[Fic] — dc20   92-10681
                                               CIP
                                               AC

For Rachel

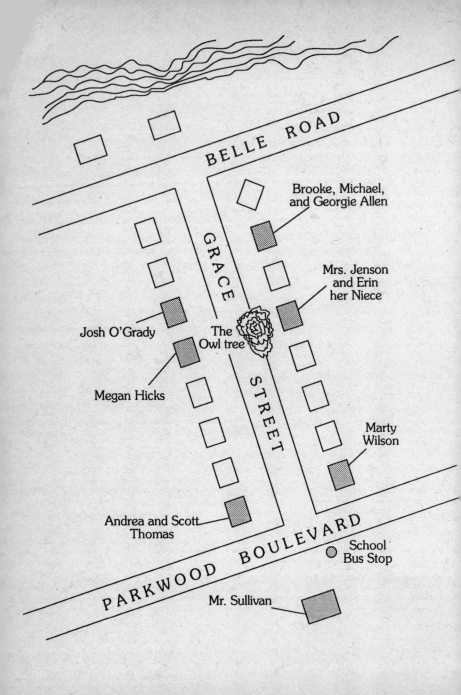

BELLE ROAD

Brooke, Michael,
and Georgie Allen

GRACE

Mrs. Jenson
and Erin
her Niece

Josh O'Grady

The
Owl tree

Megan Hicks

STREET

Marty
Wilson

Andrea and Scott
Thomas

School
Bus Stop

PARKWOOD BOULEVARD

Mr. Sullivan

Chapter One

Marty looked down. The ground below looked like the Matchbox village her brother Jack had played with when he was eleven and she was just a baby. Today, Marty was eleven and Jack was piloting the little airplane that carried them, bumping and bouncing, over Parkwood subdivision.

"Can you see Grace Street?" he asked, shouting to be heard above the whine of the engine.

"I don't know."

"Look to your right."

"There's the Owl Tree!" Marty squealed as she spotted the huge oak that stood in the middle of the block.

Jack grinned. "Happy birthday, T.J."

"Thanks, Jack. This is the best birthday present ever!"

"Want to fly over the city?"

"The city! Can we?"

"Why not? This may be the last time I'll get to fly for a while. Let's make the most of it."

Marty watched as concrete and brick replaced the neat houses and lawns of the suburbs. The closer they came to heart of the city, the closer the buildings were placed, until they stood shoulder-to-shoulder along the silvery strips of pavement. Even on Saturday, tiny cars and trucks flowed in a steady stream through the asphalt valleys separating the skyscrapers downtown. Marty sighed.

"You OK?" asked Jack.

"Yes."

"I warned you it would be bumpy. Do you feel sick at your stomach?"

"No, Jack, I love it! It's so pretty up here!"

Jack's face relaxed into a smile. "I know. Once I take off, I don't ever want to land."

He guided the plane into a wide, lazy turn and they headed back, away from the city. "Want to know a secret?"

Marty nodded.

"You have to promise not to tell Dad."

"I promise."

"I'm trying to find a job as a pilot."

"But I thought you were going to work with Dad."

"That's what he thinks, too. That's why you can't tell him."

"Don't you want to work with Dad?"

"That's not the point. I love Dad. But selling real estate is what *he's* good at, not what *I'm* good at. And it's not what I want to do. Wilson & Son Realty is his dream, not mine."

"How do you know?"

"How do I know what?"

"How do you—and other people—know what they want to do?"

"Oh. Well, they base it on what they're good

at, and what they like to do. I like to fly so I want to be a pilot. I *don't* want to be a real estate agent because I don't like selling. I'm not good at it."

"But what if you're not good at anything?"

"Everybody's good at something."

"Then, what if you don't *know* what you're good at?"

"We're not talking about 'everybody,' are we?" asked Jack. "We're talking about *you*."

Marty frowned and looked out the window. The runway of the small, suburban airport stretched out before them. Jack dipped the nose of the plane and the ground seemed to grow, expanding like the words on a balloon being filled with air. The wheels touched the runway with a jolt and a squeal. As they taxied to the hangar, Marty felt sad that the ride was over.

After they were headed home in Jack's van, he asked, "OK, T.J., what's this all about?"

"What?" asked Marty, trying to sound innocent.

"You know 'what.' Why do you think you're not good at anything?"

"Because I'm not."

"That isn't true. You're good at lots of things."

"Name one."

Jack hesitated, frowning a little.

"See?" Marty challenged.

"Wait a minute." Suddenly his face lit up. "You've always been the best reader in your class!"

"Big deal."

"It *is* a big deal. And you were the best speller in the third grade, remember?"

"Jack," sighed Marty, "I'm not talking about stuff like that."

"Then what *are* you talking about?"

"Well, dancing, like Brooke. Or singing, like Scott. Andrea can draw. Michael can act. I can't do any of those things."

"But what you *can* do is just as important. You're creative in a different way, that's all."

Marty didn't see anything creative about being a good speller or reader. "You don't understand," she told him glumly.

"Yes, I do. Your friends on Grace Street can do things you can't. So what? You can do things they can't do. That's how it works. We're all different and that's good."

She decided not to argue. Jack was her brother; he'd think she was smart and talented no matter what she said!

When they got home, Jack stopped the van halfway down the driveway instead of parking in his usual spot around back. Then he walked with Marty to the front door, jingling his keys all the way. On the porch, he stepped back and waited for her to go inside. Marty knew something was going on.

"What's wrong?"

Jack shrugged. "Nothing."

"Where are you going?"

"In the house, if you'll open the door!"

Marty looked from Jack to the van, then back at Jack. He reached around her and pulled the storm door open.

"Well?" he insisted.

Marty reached for the latch and opened the front door. As she stepped inside, the house exploded with shouts of "Surprise!" and the happy sounds of whistles and buzzers and horns. Marty's mom gave her a big hug.

"Happy birthday, honey!"

Grace Street Kids stood all around the living room, grinning and cheering. Crepe paper draped the room. Streamers dipped from window to window and across to the tulip-shaped light fixture in the middle of the ceiling. In front of the sofa, the coffee table held a pile of presents wrapped in brightly colored paper and bows. Marty smiled back. "Thanks, Mom."

"Were you surprised?" asked Andrea Thomas.

"She was surprised," Andrea's brother, Scott, told her.

Georgie Allen grabbed Marty's arm. "How was the airplane ride?"

They all crowded around—Georgie's brother Michael and her sister Brooke, Megan Hicks, Josh O'Grady, Andrea and Scott Thomas—and begged Marty to tell them all about it.

"It was great!" she began, and described every detail.

"Man," said Josh filled with awe, "I wish I could fly!"

"Me, too," agreed Georgie.

"I mean fly the airplane," said Josh, "be the pilot."

"Girls can fly airplanes, too, Josh O'Grady!" Georgie was quick to tell him.

"Careful there, Josh," agreed Jack. "One of the best pilots in my class was a woman."

"Amelia Earhart was a woman," Marty told him.

Josh looked innocent. "Who?"

"You know," said Megan. "We studied Amelia Earhart last year, remember?"

"No," said Josh slowly, shaking his head, "I don't think so."

"She was the first woman to fly across the Atlantic Ocean." Marty reminded him.

"He knows that," insisted Megan, giving Josh a shove.

"OK, OK," laughed Josh, "I know. But a man did it first!"

"So what?" asked Marty. "The woman flew faster!"

Josh opened his mouth, then closed it again and looked at Jack.

"She's right," said Jack. "It took Charles Lindbergh over thirty-three hours to make the trip. Amelia Earhart did it in less than fifteen."

"Time for presents," announced Marty's mom. "Everyone find a seat. Marty, you sit here, on the sofa."

While the kids were finding places to sit down, Marty leaned close to Jack's ear and whispered, "Thanks."

"For what?"

"For not telling Josh that Charles Lindbergh flew twice as far as Amelia Earhart!"

Jack grinned. "My pleasure."

Marty's birthday gifts were as different as the kids who had brought them. Georgie gave her the mystery novel she had been wanting, then asked to borrow it when Marty was finished reading it. Andrea gave her a pink sweater. Marty hated pink, but she pretended to love the sweater anyway. Megan and Brooke had pooled their money to buy her a trivia game.

"Megan picked it out," said Brooke. "I wanted to get the one about movies and stuff."

"It's perfect," Marty told her. "I love it!"

"Open mine next," said Michael, handing her a red and yellow package.

Marty ripped the paper off. "Extra trivia cards! Thanks, Michael!"

Scott's present was small, wrapped in green, with a matching green ribbon. He had made a tape of some of her favorite songs.

"Andrea told me what you like," he said, "and my dad fixed it so I could use a real recording studio."

"You mean, this is you singing?" she asked, holding up the tape.

Scott nodded. "My dad got a friend of his to play the guitar— nobody famous, but he's really good."

"That's so cool!" said Marty. "Thanks, Scott."

"It's not, you know, *real*, or anything, but it's OK."

"It's great! Let's listen to it."

"Wait a minute!" complained Josh.

Marty was about to stand, but sat back down and looked at him.

"You haven't opened my present, yet," he reminded her.

Marty grinned and tore into the last package on the table. It was a *rock*! She picked it up, turned it over, and inspected it closely. There was no doubt about it. It was definitely a rock!

Josh laughed. "Keep looking."

Marty looked inside the box. Taped to the bottom was an envelope. Inside was a gift certificate from her favorite Christian bookstore. She smiled at Josh.

"That's so you can buy a *good* tape," he said, "when you get tired of listening to Scott's!"

Scott shoved him and everybody laughed.

"Happy birthday to you," sang Marty's mom, coming in from the kitchen. The cake she carried had eleven burning candles.

The kids joined in and sang "Happy Birthday" to Marty. Her mom set the cake on the table in front of her. It was coconut, her favorite.

"Make a wish," said her mom.

Marty closed her eyes and thought, "I wish I had a special talent," then blew out all the candles with a single breath.

Chapter Two

"Why does he call you 'T.J.'?" asked Andrea.

"Because her middle name is Jane," said Georgie, before Marty could answer.

"Then why doesn't he call her 'M.J.'?"

Marty giggled. "That's pig latin for Jim!"

Georgie and Andrea laughed, too. The three of them were in Marty's room on Sunday afternoon, sprawled on her bed with their history books. Andrea grabbed a pillow.

"No pillow fights!" said Marty quickly.

"Then tell me," warned Andrea, holding the big down pillow above her head, ready to strike.

"OK, OK! He used to call me 'Marty J.,' then he just shortened it to T.J."

Andrea lowered the pillow. "Oh!"

"I think it's cute," said Georgie.

"I think *he's* cute," said Andrea.

Marty grinned. "You can't like Jack. He's too old!"

"He just graduated from college," agreed Georgie. "He's practically a grown-up!"

"So?" asked Andrea. "I still think he's cute."

"OK," said Marty with a shrug, "I'll tell him for you."

Andrea's eyes widened. "Don't you dare!"

Marty laughed and Andrea tossed the pillow in her face.

"Hey!" she complained. "I said no pillow fights."

"So don't throw it back," laughed Andrea.

Marty put the pillow in her lap and picked up her notebook. "What are we going to do for Black History Month?"

"I wish we could work together," said Andrea, "like we did for the Science Fair."

"Me, too," agreed Georgie.

"So do I," said Marty, "but we can't. I'm doomed."

"Why?" asked Andrea.

"Because this is supposed to be special, and I can't *do* anything special!"

"Sure, you can," said Georgie. "You did most of the research on protective coloration and you wrote descriptions of the animals for our Science Fair project. That was special."

"The *picture* of the animals was special, the part you and Andrea did. My paper just explained things."

"That was important, too," said Andrea.

"But not *special*," Marty insisted.

"Then I didn't do anything special, either," said Georgie. "All I did was paint the picture after Andrea drew it."

"But the whole thing was your idea in the first place," Marty reminded her. "I bet you already know what you're going to do for Black History Month, don't you?"

When Georgie wouldn't look at her, Marty knew she was right. "I knew it! What are you going to do?"

"It's not for sure," said Georgie cautiously, "but I might write a story."

"Like a short story?" asked Andrea.

Georgie nodded.

"I didn't know you wrote stories," said Marty, wondering why her best friend since kindergarten had never shared them with her.

"I don't," said Georgie. "I mean, I never have, but Michael gave me a diary for Christmas and I've been writing stuff. And, well, it's fun! So I thought I'd try a story."

"What's it about?" asked Marty.

"Remember Harriet Tubman, the woman who led all those slaves to freedom on the Underground Railroad?"

Marty nodded. "It's about her?"

"Not really," said Georgie. "It's about a little girl on one of those trips. I'm writing it like it's her diary."

"See?" Marty asked Andrea. "She always has the best ideas. And she can write, too!"

"You haven't read it, yet," Georgie reminded her.

"Oh, it'll be good!" said Marty. "And Andrea will draw something really cool, and I'll be in the fifth grade forever because I won't have a project!"

"Don't worry," said Georgie. "We'll help you think of something."

"It's five o'clock," said Jack from the open doorway.

"Thanks, Jack," said Georgie, gathering up her books.

Andrea just sat there, grinning at Jack. Marty poked her. "I thought you had to leave at five, too."

"Oh, right," said Andrea, sounding startled. She grabbed her books and followed Georgie from the room.

"What's wrong with *her*?" asked Jack.

"She thinks you're cute," said Marty, "but I'm not supposed to tell."

Jack grinned. "Oh, I see. Did you get your homework done?"

"No. We never do when we study together. Don't tell Mom, though."

"I won't, but you *will* finish your homework, right?"

"I can do it after church tonight. Jack?"

"What?"

"Nothing. Just . . ." She wanted to ask him why he didn't go to church anymore. Instead, she said, "I had a great birthday yesterday."

Jack smiled at her. "I'm glad. Supper's almost ready. Mom wants you to come and set the table."

"OK."

Sunday suppers were usually sandwiches and soup. Sometimes her dad made his special venison chili with beans. Marty liked it if she pretended she wasn't eating deer meat. She checked the pot on the stove. It was vegetable soup.

"Where's Dad?"

Her mom handed her a tray of chicken sandwiches to put on the table. "He's at work."

"On Sunday?"

"He had an open house this afternoon."

"Oh." Marty set a place for him anyway, but he didn't come home until she and her mom were leaving for church.

"Do you want us to wait for you?" her mom asked him.

"No, you two go ahead," he told her, then looked at Marty. "You can tell me all about it when you get back."

After they were in the car, Marty asked, "Why didn't Dad come to church with us?"

"He was just tired, sweetheart. He's been so busy lately."

"Is that why Jack quit going?"

"I don't know what's happened to Jack. It's as if he left the church behind when he went off to college."

"Does he still believe in God?"

"Of course he does! And now that he's back home, we'll get him going to church again. You'll see. And your dad won't be so tired all the time because he'll have Jack to help him with the business."

Marty bit her lower lip and reminded herself to keep quiet. She wondered, though—what if

Jack *did* get a job as a pilot and moved away again? Would that mean he'd *never* go back to church?

Marty's church was small. When it was built, it was out in the country, surrounded by pastures and hay fields. Now the growing town had edged closer, and both city and farm families enjoyed worshiping together.

Marty liked the little church. She liked having one big Sunday school class, where she was asked to help the younger children with their Bible lessons. She liked the worship services, too. Pastor Hollis preached to the tiny congregation as if he were delivering the Sermon on the Mount to thousands of listeners. Sometimes his voice rattled the windows. Other times, he spoke so softly that Marty had to lean forward to hear him. Sometimes he used words she didn't understand. But even so, she always liked his preaching.

Sometimes on Sunday nights, Pastor Hollis would decide not to preach so they could use the whole hour to "praise the Lord with song!" Marty liked the fact that every member sang, from the youngest child to old Mr. Billingsly, who was always two words behind everybody else.

"Do you think Pastor Hollis will preach tonight?" she asked her mom as they pulled into the parking lot beside the church.

"I don't know. Why?"

"Just wondering." It really didn't matter. Either way, singing or listening to Pastor Hollis, she'd be able to stop thinking about Jack and special talents and Black History Month projects for a while.

As they entered the building, a half dozen children aged five to seven flocked to Marty's side. She smiled at them and listened to their chatter until their moms called them to go into the sanctuary for vespers. Marty and her mom sat near the front.

After the hymns, Pastor Hollis read 1 Corinthians 12:4-7. Marty listened carefully as he explained that gifts are given by the Holy Spirit to each one for the common good. Pastor Hollis continued to talk about the "common good," but Marty kept thinking about "each one." The Scripture had said "each one" had a spiritual gift—"each one," including her!

Chapter Three

At the bus stop on Parkwood the next morning, Marty met Georgie and Andrea. They had hardly arrived when Marty said, "I'm sure I have a spiritual gift."

"What's a spiritual gift?" asked Andrea.

"It's like a talent," said Marty, "that you use for the church."

"Oh."

"Don't you get it?"

"I get it," said Georgie. "It means you have a

31

special talent, just like we've been saying all along."

"Except you didn't believe us," Andrea pointed out.

"I know," admitted Marty, "but if the Bible says it, I *have* to believe it!"

"Does the Bible say how to find out what it is?" asked Georgie.

"I don't think so," said Marty, "but the Holy Spirit gives it to you. Maybe the Spirit is supposed to tell you."

"How?" asked Andrea.

"I don't know."

"Maybe you could just try a bunch of different things," suggested Georgie.

"Right!" agreed Andrea. "Then when you find something you're good at, you'll know that's it!"

"Sounds like I'm right back where I started," said Marty glumly.

"But you're not," insisted Georgie, "because now you know you *have* a talent."

Marty thought about it. "Maybe you're right," she said finally. "My mom says the Holy Spirit guides us. Maybe if I try some things, He'll guide me to my talent. OK, I'll do it! What should I try first?"

"I could teach you to draw," Andrea offered.

"How about writing?" asked Georgie.

"I'll try both!" said Marty. "When do we start?"

"Right after school," said Georgie.

They met at Georgie's house. Andrea brought some drawing paper and colored pencils. Marty sat at Georgie's desk and drew a horse.

"That's great!" said Andrea. "See? You've found your gift already!"

"Aren't giraffes supposed to be sort of orange?" asked Georgie.

"It's a horse," said Marty.

Andrea looked more closely at the picture. "It is?"

"Maybe we should try something else," suggested Marty.

"Let's try writing," said Georgie. "You always get A's on your research papers."

"OK."

Georgie gave her some notebook paper and a

pencil. Marty looked at the sheet of paper. "What should I write?"

"Anything you want," said Georgie.

Marty stared at the paper again. Her mind was as blank as the page in front of her. "I can't think of anything."

"Write about Dr. King," suggested Andrea. "We just studied him."

"OK."

Marty wrote down everything she could remember about Dr. Martin Luther King, Jr. When she had filled the page, she handed the paper to Georgie and waited anxiously while she read it.

"Maybe we should start with something easier," said Georgie, passing the paper to Andrea.

"What's wrong with it?" asked Marty.

"Nothing. It's just . . ."

"Boring," said Andrea.

"It's not boring," said Georgie, frowning at Andrea. "It's just, you know, facts."

"How did you remember all this stuff?" asked Andrea.

Marty shrugged. "I don't know. We talked about it in class."

"Do you remember what Dr. King looked like?" asked Georgie.

"Sure," said Marty. "We watched a tape of some of his speeches."

"OK," said Georgie, "then pretend like you met him today, and write about that."

"What do you mean?"

"Pretend you were walking down Grace Street and you met him."

"*Now*, today," asked Marty, "or when he was alive, today?"

"What?"

"Do you mean pretend he's still alive or pretend I live in the sixties?"

"Never mind," said Georgie.

"No, wait," said Marty. "I think I can do this . . ."

"Maybe Scott can teach you to sing," interrupted Andrea.

"I love to sing."

"Great!" said Georgie. "Let's go find Scott."

January on Grace Street usually meant snow. This year, the temperature hovered just above freezing. Heavy gray clouds hung low in the sky. When Marty stepped outside, a light breeze lifted her short blonde hair.

"Those look like snow clouds," she said.

"It's not cold enough," argued Georgie.

"I hope it doesn't rain again," said Andrea.

"Are you sure Scott's at your house?" Marty asked her.

"He was there when I left," said Andrea. "Michael was with him."

"Do you think he'll mind?"

"What? Teaching you to sing?"

Marty nodded. "I listened to his tape. He's really good."

"He won't mind," said Andrea. "He likes showing off how good he is."

"Michael's a pretty good actor," said Georgie. "If the singing doesn't work, we can try that."

"OK," said Marty. She was ready to try anything.

Suddenly, Josh O'Grady whipped around them on his skateboard and roared down the sidewalk. He stepped back on the board, spun around, and stopped in front of them.

"Hi, Josh," said Marty.

"Hi. What's up?"

"Nothing. We're going to Andrea's house."

"Oh."

"Scott's going to teach Marty to sing," said Andrea.

"How come?" asked Josh.

"We're trying to find something she's good at," said Andrea.

"Andrea!" warned Georgie.

"It's OK," said Marty. "It's true."

"Maybe you're good at sports," suggested Josh. "Try this."

Josh kicked the skateboard with the toe of his sneaker and it rolled across the concrete to Marty's feet.

"I don't think so," she said doubtfully.

"It won't hurt to try," said Josh.

"It will if I fall off!" said Marty.

"Come on, Marty," said Andrea nudging her friend. "You said you wanted to try different things."

Marty looked at Georgie, who shrugged. "It *is* different!"

"I'll help you," said Josh. "You won't fall off."

Marty sighed. "Show me what to do."

Josh stood behind her and held her hands while she balanced on the skateboard. Georgie and Andrea stood a few feet down the sidewalk, ready to catch her if she fell. When she felt steady, she nodded her head and Josh gave the skateboard a little push.

It rolled slowly at first, and Marty's outstretched arms kept her balanced. As the board picked up speed, though, Marty began to wobble. Waving her arms frantically, she was barely able to keep her footing. Suddenly, the sidewalk curved to the left, the board went straight, and Marty flew off to the right. She landed on the curb with her right arm bent behind her back.

"Marty!" screamed Georgie and Andrea together, and rushed to help her up.

"You were supposed to catch me," she reminded them.

"Are you OK?" asked Josh, running to her side.

"I think so. Did I hurt your skateboard?"

"The board's fine," he assured her.

Marty looked around. The skateboard was sitting innocently upright on a patch of brown grass. Then she straightened her right arm and pain shot from her elbow to her shoulder. Marty yelled and grabbed her arm with her left hand.

"What's wrong?" asked Georgie.

"My arm," said Marty through clenched teeth.

"It's my fault," said Josh.

"I bet it's broken," said Andrea.

Georgie put her arm around Marty. "Is your mom home?"

Marty nodded.

"We should call 911," said Josh.

"Her mom's a nurse," Georgie told him.

They huddled around Marty like Secret Service agents guarding the president, and walked her home. Marty's mom was in the kitchen.

"What happened?" she asked.

"I hurt my arm," said Marty.

"It was my fault," said Josh miserably.

Marty's mom took her arm and gently bent the elbow. "Does that hurt?"

Marty shook her head. When her mom stretched out her arm, though, she winced with pain.

"I don't think it's broken," said her mom, "but we'd better have it X-rayed, just to be sure."

"I'm sorry, Marty," said Josh.

"It wasn't your fault," she told him.

"It was my skateboard."

"You were riding a skateboard?" asked her mom.

"I don't think I actually rode it," said Marty. "Mostly, I just fell off!"

Her mom laughed. "Don't worry, Josh. She's going to be fine."

The kids walked with Marty to the car. Just before she closed the door, Georgie leaned over and whispered in Marty's ear, "At least now we know your gift isn't sports!"

Chapter Four

Marty went to school on Tuesday with her elbow wrapped in an elastic bandage. She had talked her mom out of making her wear a sling, but she kept her arm tucked up against her waist and remembered to use her left hand for everything.

"It's not broken," she told Josh at the bus stop. "It's just sprained."

"Does it hurt?"

"Not all the time, but it hurts when I move it."

"I guess we should have skipped the sports and gone straight to the singing," said Andrea.

Marty laughed, and something floated past the corner of her eye. She looked around and something landed on her eyelashes. Suddenly, she understood. She held out her hand and caught a snowflake on her red mitten.

"It's snowing!"

"Sort of," said Josh.

He was right. There weren't many flakes in the air, but the sky was dark and gray, and a cold wind stung Marty's eyes.

"I bet it snows before lunchtime," she told him.

By noon, however, streaks of rosy sunlight were beginning to show around the edges of the clouds. Marty scowled as she sat down with Georgie and Andrea in the school cafeteria.

"What's wrong with you?" asked Andrea.

"Is your arm hurting?" asked Georgie.

"No," said Marty, "I'm mad. Why won't it snow?"

Andrea shrugged. "Who cares?"

"I do!"

"Me, too," said Georgie. "We haven't had any snow all winter."

"That's fine with me," said Andrea. "I hate snow."

Marty stared at her. "How can you hate snow?"

"Easy. It's wet and it's cold and it's messy . . . I hate it!"

Marty didn't know what to say. She had never known anyone who hated snow before, except grown-ups.

"Hey, I think I know what I'm going to do for Black History Month," said Andrea.

"What?" asked Georgie.

"My dad's got a bunch of old magazines, from the 1960s. He said I could have them to make a collage about the civil rights movement. What do you think?"

"I think it's great!" said Georgie.

"Yeah, great," echoed Marty, without enthusiasm.

"What's wrong with it?" asked Andrea.

"Nothing!" said Marty. She knew she was

almost shouting, but couldn't stop herself. "It's great! *You've* got a great idea! *Georgie's* got a great idea! *Everybody's* got a great idea! So what's wrong with *me*?!"

Georgie and Andrea stared at her, unable to speak. Marty blushed. Her face felt hot and her eyes watered.

"Sorry," she told them.

"You *never* get mad," said Georgie softly, puzzled over Marty's outburst.

"She just did," Andrea pointed out.

"I didn't mean to," said Marty.

"It's OK," said Georgie. "We told you we'd help you think of something for your project."

"I know."

"And we'll help you find your gift, too," said Andrea.

Marty forced a smile. "Thanks."

"But we just can't make it snow!" said Georgie.

Marty smiled for real.

When she got home from school that afternoon, Jack was sitting in the den watching television.

"Hi, Jack," she greeted him. "What are you doing here?"

"Hi, T.J. I live here!"

Marty giggled.

Jack grinned. "Dad gave me the rest of the afternoon off so I could be here when you got home."

"Where's Mom?"

"The hospital called her in. How's your arm?"

"It's OK. Can I go over to Andrea's? Scott's going to teach me to sing."

"To sing? Why?"

"Remember when you said everybody's good at something?"

Jack nodded.

"Well, it's true. The Bible says everyone has a gift."

"And you think yours might be singing?"

"I don't know. Maybe."

Jack sighed. "I guess it's OK. Would Mom let you go?"

"Yes."

"Really?"

"Really. It's just across the street."

"All right. I'll be here if you need me."

"Thanks, Jack."

Marty ran across Grace Street to Andrea's house. Michael and Georgie were already there. Scott had his CD player set up in the living room and they were listening to Amy Grant. When Scott sang along with the chorus, it sounded like part of the recording.

"Do you know this song?" he asked Marty.

She nodded. It was one of her favorites.

"Sing with me next time."

At the chorus, Marty began to sing. It didn't sound like part of the recording. It didn't sound much like singing!

"I sound better at church," she told him.

"OK," said Scott, switching off the CD, "let's sing a hymn. What do you like?"

"Amazing Grace."

Scott started the hymn and everyone joined in. Marty sang as if she were in her little church, praising His grace to the top of her voice. When the song ended, she looked at Scott. He was frowning.

"Not bad," he said slowly.

"But not good, either," she guessed.

"Maybe we should try acting," said Georgie.

Everybody looked at Michael.

"Me?" he asked. "I can't act!"

"Yes, you can," said Scott.

"You're a good actor," agreed Georgie.

"I was in one pageant," said Michael.

"And you had the leading role," said Scott.

"Please, Michael?" Marty begged.

Michael sighed. "OK."

Andrea got one of her novels. They found a scene with a lot of dialog between two people. Michael and Marty read the scene aloud together.

"That was pretty good," said Michael, "but you sound like you're acting."

"Isn't that what we're doing?" asked Marty.

"Yes, but it's not supposed to sound like it."

"Oh." Marty had a sinking feeling that acting wasn't going to work out either.

"Let's try it again," said Michael, "and this time, try not to think about yourself. Only think about the character."

Marty did her best, but even she could tell that it sounded worse than the first time.

"Maybe you're just trying too hard," said Michael.

"Maybe I just can't act," said Marty. "Thanks, anyway."

"Have you tried dancing?" he asked. "Brooke could show you some steps."

"I think I'll skip dancing," she said, gently rubbing her sprained elbow. "It sounds a lot like sports to me!"

Marty went home feeling that she was no closer to finding her gift than when she first started looking. As she pushed open the front door, she heard loud voices coming from the den. Quietly, she closed the door and stood in front of it, listening. Her dad was home, and he and Jack were arguing.

"All of a sudden, you don't want anything to do with it!" he shouted. "Just like that, you'd throw away everything we've worked for!"

Jack's voice was lower, calmer. "It's not 'just like that.' You've always known I wanted to fly."

"But here, for the company. I thought having

your pilot's license would be good for the business."

"I'm not happy just having the license, Dad. I want to use it. I want to be a pilot."

"We're not talking about being happy. We're talking about a job!"

There was a long pause. Marty held her breath. She knew she shouldn't be listening, but if she went to her room, she'd have to go past the den.

"You can't mean that," said Jack. "Doesn't your job make you happy?"

"Not lately," their dad said quietly. "I'm sorry, Jack. Of course I want you to be happy."

"I know."

Marty sighed and walked to the den door.

"Hi, T.J.," said Jack.

"Hi, pumpkin," said her dad. He sounded tired and looked embarrassed. "How was your day?"

"Just fine," she said trying to smile. "What's for supper?"

"Supper?"

"I'll order a pizza," said Jack, heading for the telephone.

Marty went to her dad and gave him a one-arm hug.

"How's the arm?" he asked.

"It's OK."

"Been staying away from skateboards?"

Marty grinned and her dad winked at her. Suddenly, his eyebrows shot up. "Oh, guess what!"

"What?"

"You know that big house over on Crestwood?"

Marty nodded. "The one the country music singer owns."

"Well, she wants me to sell it for her."

"You signed the Crestlawn estate?" asked Jack, hanging up the phone.

Marty's dad nodded. "This afternoon."

"Can we go look at it?" asked Marty.

"It won't be vacant until the end of the week."

"*Then* can we go?"

Her dad laughed. "OK. Friday afternoon we'll go look at Crestlawn."

Chapter Five

Crestlawn!" said Andrea in science class the next day. "You're so lucky! I'd *love* to see Crestlawn!"

"I heard it's got a bowling alley in the basement," said Georgie.

"And an indoor swimming pool," said Andrea.

"And a movie theater!" said Georgie.

"A movie theater?" asked Marty doubtfully.

"Well, maybe not a theater," said Georgie,

"but, you know, a screening room. That's what Brooke told me, anyway."

"Take us with you," Andrea begged Marty.

"Please?" added Georgie.

"If I do," said Marty, "you can't tell anybody else. My dad won't take us if the whole street shows up!"

"We won't tell," said Andrea.

"We promise," said Georgie.

"OK," said Marty, "you can go."

Georgie and Andrea held back squeals of delight as their science teacher, Mr. Prescott, strolled over.

"Am I going to have to send you girls to separate learning stations?" he asked.

"No, sir," they answered together.

"Then let's get our minds back on weather fronts, shall we?"

"Yes, sir."

Marty turned her attention back to the learning center in front of them. They were seated at a small table that was pushed up against the back wall of the classroom. On the wall, above the table, hung a bulletin board with displays of weather maps and satellite pictures. The table held a video monitor and VCR, reference books, some newspapers, and a black loose-leaf notebook.

Marty opened the notebook. The plastic-covered pages contained instructions for using the learning center. Step one was to start the VCR and watch a tape about weather fronts. Marty pushed the *play* button.

After school, Marty sat with Georgie on the bus. Andrea took the seat in front of them and sat sideways, so she could talk to them.

"What was the one with the little pointy cold front marks and the little round warm front marks, all on the same curved line?" she asked.

"It's called a stationary front," Marty told her.

"That's the one I don't understand," said Andrea. "How can you have a warm front and a cold front at the same time?"

"Because the warm air mass and the cold air mass are both strong," said Marty. "Neither one can move so the front is stationary."

"That means standing in one place," said Georgie.

"I know what stationary means," said Andrea.

"Yeah, not moving," said Marty, "like me."

"What do you mean?" asked Georgie.

"I mean I still haven't found my talent," Marty complained.

"We'll find it," said Georgie.

"But when? It's almost February and I still don't know what to do for Black History Month!"

"You know a lot about Dr. King," said Andrea. "Maybe you could do a project about him."

"What kind of project?"

"I don't know," admitted Andrea.

"Dr. King always wanted to be a preacher," said Marty. "Even when he was a little boy, he knew what he wanted to be."

"Just like Brooke," said Georgie, "with dancing, I mean."

Marty nodded. "I know, and Jack has always wanted to be a pilot. How come everybody knows what they want to be, except me?"

"I don't know what I want to be," said Georgie.

"Me neither," said Andrea.

"Really?" Marty looked closely at their faces to see if they were just being nice.

"Really," insisted Georgie.

Then Marty remembered. "But you know what your talent is," she said, her spirits sinking again. "You both do."

The bus stopped at the end of Grace Street and let the kids out on the corner by Marty's house.

"Do you want to come over?" asked Andrea.

"I can't," said Marty. "I have to do my homework so I can go to church tonight."

"Mom?" shouted Marty as she opened the front door.

"She's at the hospital. She had to work late again," Jack called from the den.

Marty went into the den. Jack was stretched out on the sofa reading a book.

"Hi, Jack."

"Hi, T.J. How was school today?"

Marty shrugged. "OK, I guess. How was work?"

"Fine."

"How's Dad?" she asked casually.

Jack closed the book and sat up. "You heard, didn't you, T.J.?"

"Heard what?"

"Dad and me. You heard us arguing last night, didn't you?"

Marty nodded.

"I thought so. Come here."

Marty went over and sat next to him on the sofa.

"I told him I was going to be a pilot," said Jack.

"And he got mad?"

"He was just disappointed."

"He sounded mad."

Jack grinned. "Well, maybe he was a little mad. But mostly he was disappointed. He was counting on me to work for him, and he really needs the help right now."

"Why? What's wrong?"

"Nothing's wrong. That's just it—business is so good he can't handle it all."

"Are you going to help him?"

"I will until I can find a job flying. After that,

62

he'll have to hire somebody else, whether he likes it or not!"

By the time Marty finished her homework and went into the kitchen to check on supper, her dad still wasn't home. Jack was pulling a casserole out of the oven.

"You're just in time," he told her as he set the steaming dish on the kitchen table. Only two places were set.

"When's Dad coming home?" she asked.

"He'll be late. Why?"

"I was going to ask him to take me to church tonight."

"I'll take you."

"You will?"

Jack laughed. "Did you think I wouldn't?"

"I didn't think you liked to go to church anymore."

"It's not that," said Jack, spooning chicken casserole onto her plate. "I guess I just got out of the habit."

Marty didn't understand. She thought you

either went to church, or you didn't. She had never thought of it as a habit.

"The casserole's safe," said Jack with a grin. "Mom made it before she went to work."

"What?"

"Your food. You were staring at your plate like you thought I was trying to poison you!"

"Oh." Marty grinned, too, and took a bite of chicken.

On Wednesday nights, Pastor Hollis held a Bible study class for the adults, while the kids had their youth meetings. The junior high and senior high students met together in one group. The other kids, first through sixth graders, met in another group. Some of them complained, but Marty like meeting with the younger children. Her group leader, Mrs. Cole, let her plan puppet shows and Bible games for them.

"Did I see Jack come in with you?" asked Mrs. Cole when Marty got to class that night.

"Yes, he's home from college now."

"Well, it's nice to have him back at church."

"Mrs. Cole?"

"Yes?"

"Jack says going to church is a habit. Is that true?"

"I suppose it is—a good habit."

"But Pastor Hollis says you should *want* to go to church."

"Yes," said Mrs. Cole, frowning a little, "that's true, too. Sometimes, though, we go to church even when we don't feel like it. Have you ever done that?"

"I guess so."

"Why didn't you just say, 'I don't feel like going,' and stay home?"

"I don't know."

"I do. It's because you've made a habit of going to church. And you know what else? I'll bet that once you got there, you were glad you went."

Marty grinned.

Mrs. Cole patted her on the back, then turned her attention to the other children who were beginning to fill the room.

Chapter Six

On Friday morning, Marty's teacher let them go to the library to work on their projects for Black History Month.

"What am I supposed to work on?" whispered Andrea. "All my magazines are at home."

"What about me?" asked Marty. "I don't even have a project yet!"

"I wish Georgie was in our regular class," said Andrea, "and not just our science class."

"Me, too."

"Shh," said the librarian.

Marty found two books about Martin Luther King, Jr., and tried to read, but Andrea kept asking her questions.

"Are we still going this afternoon? Did you ask your dad? Is it OK if Georgie and I come, too? What if it snows? Will we still go if it snows?"

"Shh!" said the librarian. She glared at them from the shelves where she was helping someone.

Marty wished it *would* snow! The sky was gloomy and a few flakes slipped past the windows now and then, just as it had the other day. But every time, the clouds broke up and the sun came out before much snow could fall.

By lunchtime it was snowing. By the time school was out, the ground was white. The snow was melting off the roads, though, and the bus had no trouble getting them safely back to Grace Street.

"Are we still going to Crestlawn?" asked Andrea.

"Probably," said Marty. "Let's go ask Dad."

"I need to go home first," said Georgie.

"Me, too," said Andrea. "Go ask him and we'll be there in a few minutes."

"OK."

Marty ran through the thin blanket of snow to her front porch. Stamping her feet to clean her boots, she opened the front door with her key and went inside.

"Dad?"

"It's me again," said Jack, meeting her in the hallway.

"Where's Dad?"

"What do you mean, 'Where's Dad?' He's at work."

"But he was going to take us to see Crestlawn this afternoon."

Jack sighed and ran his fingers through his blonde hair. "I guess he forgot, T.J."

"I invited Georgie and Andrea," said Marty, almost crying.

"Tell you what. I'll check Dad's desk. If the key's there, I'll take you for a quick look at the place."

Marty beamed. "Thanks, Jack!"

She followed him to her parents' bedroom and

held her breath while he searched the desk. He found the Crestlawn keys in the bottom drawer.

Jack grabbed his parka and they went out the back door. Georgie and Andrea were waiting beside the van. So were Brooke, Michael, Scott, and Megan.

"You promised!" Marty scolded Georgie.

"I didn't say a word," said Georgie. "Honest!"

Marty looked at Andrea. "Then how did they find out?"

"I only told Scott," she said.

"I just told Michael," said Scott.

"I guess I told Brooke," admitted Michael.

"I had to tell Megan," said Brooke. "She's my best friend!"

Marty looked around. "Didn't anybody tell Josh? He's the only one missing."

"Well, actually . . ." began Megan. She stopped as Josh came crunching through the snow on his skateboard.

"Good thing I've got a van," said Jack.

Crestlawn was only a few miles from Parkwood subdivision, but the snow slowed them down. Halfway there, it got so dark that Jack had to turn on the headlights. In the yellow beams, the snow began to swirl in a rising wind. Jack looked worried.

"I'm beginning to think this wasn't such a good idea, T.J."

"Should we go home?" asked Marty.

He shook his head. "We've come too far. Crestlawn is closer. I just hope we make it before this stuff turns into a blizzard."

They inched along. Once they slid into the car in front of them, but they were going so slowly that no harm was done. Finally, they turned onto Crestwood. It was a two-lane, country road with no painted lines to guide them. Jack leaned forward over the wheel and squinted through the windshield. Marty looked, too. She could see the hood of the van and very little else. Suddenly Jack laughed.

"I never thought I'd be grateful for litter!" he said.

Marty followed his gaze out the front window of the van. There was a brief flash as the headlights reflected off something on the side of the road.

"What is it?" she asked.

"Soda cans would be my guess," said Jack, "but right now they're like markers to keep us out of the ditch."

He was right. By watching the flashes, Marty could tell when the road curved. Soon, a shadowy arch loomed in front of them. As they got closer, the top was lost in the swirling, white storm, but Marty knew what it said: CRESTLAWN. Jack drove under the arch and crept up the long driveway to the covered portico at the side of the house. Before he turned off the motor, Michael opened the van door and the Grace Street Kids hurried out.

Crestlawn was huge. The entrance hall was bigger than Marty's living room. The rubber soles of her boots squeaked on the marble floor. Jack flipped a switch beside the door and light filled the room.

"Good," said Jack. "The electricity's still on. Let's see if there's a telephone."

He led the way through a set of double doors to the left of the entrance hall. Marty stayed close behind him, and the rest of the kids gathered behind her. When Jack moved, they all moved.

"I think this is the living room," said Jack as he turned on the lights.

Marty gasped. They were in a room almost half the size of her school's cafeteria. There were sofas and chairs and carved, wooden tables that looked like they belonged in "Beauty and the Beast."

"Look at the furniture!" exclaimed Marty.

"The owners just took their personal things when they left," explained Jack. "The movers are coming next week to get the rest, so . . ."

"Don't touch anything," Josh finished for him.

"Right."

"There's a telephone," said Marty, pointing.

A small desk stood against the wall across. On it sat a gold and white telephone with a round base and a dainty receiver.

"That's a telephone?" asked Josh.

Jack laughed and walked to the desk. The Grace Street Kids followed him. He picked up the receiver and listened.

"We've got a dial tone," he told them. "I want you to take turns calling your parents to let them know you're all right."

"When do we say we'll be home?" asked Megan.

"We'll have to wait until the storm's over," said Jack, "and it will take them a while to get the roads cleared after that. Just tell them you're OK and you'll be here until it's safe to travel."

"Wow," said Brooke dreamily, "trapped in a blizzard."

"At Crestlawn!" said Andrea.

Marty grinned. "*This* will make a good story for your diary, Georgie!"

After the kids called their parents, Jack called their dad at work and told him where they were.

"Is he mad?" asked Marty, as he hung up the phone.

"Why would he be mad?" asked Jack.

"Because we brought *everybody!*" said Marty.

Jack grinned. "He's not mad. In fact, he said there may still be food in the pantry!"

Marty was shocked. "We can't eat their food! Can we?"

"Only if there's a blizzard outside," said Jack, "and we can't get home for supper."

"Hey, cool!" said Josh. "I wonder what a country music star eats."

"I wonder where the kitchen is," said Michael.

Jack led them back to the entrance hall and through a second set of double doors on the other side. They were in a formal dining room. The longest table Marty had ever seen occupied the center of the room. High-backed chairs circled the table and stood against the powder blue walls. There was another door at the far end of the room.

Marty, with the kids crowding behind her, followed Jack around the table, through the door, and into a smaller room with buffet tables and china cabinets. Marty laughed at herself for thinking of the room as "smaller." It was larger than the den at her house, and there was an elevator in the corner.

"Way cool!" said Scott.

"It looks like a giant bird cage," said Brooke. "What's it for?"

"It's an elevator," Marty told her, thinking it really did look like a bird cage. It reminded her of the elevators she had seen in one of the fancy hotels in the city, only this one was smaller and dropped through a round hole in the floor.

"It probably goes down to the kitchen," said Jack.

"We'll have to take turns," said Josh. "I'll bet that thing won't hold more than two people."

"There should be some stairs close by," said Jack.

They all looked around for a stairway. There were two doors besides the one they had used to enter from the dining room. Jack went to the one on the right while Marty tried the one in the back. Jack found the stairs. What Marty found took her breath away.

Behind the door was a dressing room. Beyond the dressing room, surrounded by a blue tile floor and walls of glass, was an Olympic-size swimming pool.

"It's true," she whispered, "there *is* a pool."

Chapter Seven

Marty stood beside the diving board and looked down into the water. Dark blue tile lined the sides of the pool, but the bottom was a mosaic of the ocean floor. Brightly painted fish, shells, coral, and seaweed were set against a sandy-colored background.

"It's beautiful," said Andrea, almost whispering.

Marty looked around. The kids were lined up

along the edge of the pool like swimmers about to start a race.

"I found the stairs." Jack's voice echoed off the tile and glass. "Anybody hungry?"

No one answered. They were all gazing around the room with looks of wonder. On three sides, the walls were smoke-tinted glass from floor to ceiling. Outside, Marty could see a fierce swirl of snow. She could hear the angry whistling of the wind as it threw itself against the windows. Inside, the surface of the water was perfectly still.

Josh broke the silence. "Did somebody mention food?"

Marty grinned. As if coming out of a trance, the kids began to stir. She turned to Jack. "Lead the way."

The kitchen was chrome. Sinks, counter tops, appliances—everything was chrome, Even the floor's gray tile gave the impression of walking on chrome. The refrigerators—there were three of them, and two freezers—were empty, but the pantry still held enough packaged and canned goods to feed them for a month. Marty found a jar of peanut butter.

"Peanut butter?" asked Josh, sounding disappointed.

Marty laughed. "Everybody eats peanut butter, Josh, including country music stars!"

There wasn't any bread, but Scott found some crackers and a large can of tomato juice. Marty found a can opener and knives for the peanut butter. They couldn't find any glasses so they drank the juice out of coffee mugs. Jack offered to make soup, but everyone was eager to see the rest of the house.

Next to the kitchen was a laundry room. Beyond that, at the end of a short hallway, was the game room. It ran the length of the house, from front to back, and took up nearly half the width. Light pine paneling covered the walls. The floor was carpeted with a low pile, wheat-colored rug, except for a three-foot wide strip of polished hardwood along the far wall.

"It's the bowling alley!" said Georgie.

Marty went over to the lane. It looked shorter than a regulation lane, but not by much, and was complete with gutters and ten pins. A rack of black balls stood nearby.

A half dozen arcade-style video games lined the opposite wall. One end of the room held comfortable sofas and chairs, two card tables, and several cabinets full of board games. In the corner across from the door, reaching through a round hole in the ceiling, was a spiral staircase. Marty walked to the foot of the stairs and looked up.

"That looks interesting," said Jack, close behind her.

She turned and smiled at him. "Let's go see what's up there."

Jack looked around the room. The other kids, who had stayed flocked together like sheep since arriving at Crestlawn, were now scattered everywhere playing different games.

"They'll be OK," said Marty. "Please, Jack? I'll just go look and come right back."

"I'd better go with you." Jack started up the steps. Marty took a deep breath and followed him. The lights from the game room reached only to the top of the stairs. Beyond that, she could see nothing.

"Stand still," said Jack.

She could hear his hand on the wall, searching for a switch. Suddenly, there was light.

"It's the screening room," said Marty.

Rows of black, overstuffed chairs faced a giant video screen. Thick black carpeting covered the floor and drapes of heavy black velvet lined the walls.

"No wonder it was so dark," said Jack, sinking into the soft cushions of a chair.

Marty sat next to him. "That's the biggest TV I've ever seen!"

"Me, too," laughed Jack.

"Thanks for bringing us, Jack."

"Even if we did get trapped in a blizzard?"

Marty grinned. "That's the best part!"

"I've been meaning to ask you," said Jack. "How did the singing lessons go?"

"Not great," she admitted. "In fact, I was terrible."

"I've heard you sing. You're not that bad."

"I'm not that good, either. Whatever my talent is, it's definitely not singing!"

"I think you're worrying too much about this

talent thing. You're only eleven. You've still got plenty of time to figure out what you want to do with your life."

"You don't understand."

"Yes, I do."

"No, you don't, Jack! You've *always* known what you wanted to do."

"No, I haven't."

"What?"

Marty thought she must have heard him wrong. For as long as she could remember, Jack had wanted to fly. She was sure of it.

"When I was your age, I had no idea. I used to hate it when people asked me what I wanted to be when I grew up! I didn't discover flying until I was in high school."

"Really, Jack?"

"I wouldn't lie to you."

Marty walked all the way around the big screen, trying to see how it worked, while she thought about what Jack said.

"Do you think I'll have to wait till I'm in high school to find my gift?" she asked him.

"The Bible says there's a right time for

everything, T.J. You'll find your gift when the time is right."

"When will that be?"

"I don't know. God reveals things in His own time. That's what Pastor Hollis talked about Wednesday night."

"Did you like the Bible study?"

"It was pretty good. Why?"

"Mrs. Cole says if you go to church, even when you don't feel like it, you'll be glad you went. Are you glad you went?"

Jack's blue eyes twinkled. "I suppose so. Are you now going to suggest I go to church with you Sunday morning?"

"I was just wondering," Marty said innocently.

"Right. "

Marty stood on her knees in one of the chairs and swiveled back and forth. "I like to go to church. It's like going to Grampa's house on the Fourth of July."

Jack laughed. "What?"

"You know," explained Marty. "When all the aunts and uncles and cousins are there."

"How's our family reunion like church?"

Marty made dents in the black cushion with her finger. She had thought it but had never before tried to say it out loud. "Well, I know Grampa's always there. And I can write him letters and talk to him on the phone. But it's more fun to go see him. And it's even better when the whole family's there."

"So you're saying that God is always with us, but we can feel closer to Him at His house."

"And it's the only time we get to see some of the other church people," added Marty.

Suddenly, Scott's head popped out of the stairwell.

"I found them!" he called back down to the game room, then climbed the rest of the way up. Soon, Grace Street Kids were popping up one after the other, like rabbits from a burrow.

"This is cool!" said Brooke. "What a great place to watch movies!"

"Why is everything black?" asked Michael.

"To make it dark enough for the projection screen," Brooke told him.

"What's a projection screen?" asked Georgie.

"That giant TV over there," said Marty. "It works like a film projector."

Jack stood up and looked around. "I wonder where the door is."

Marty went to the nearest wall and started working her way around the room, looking for an opening in the drapes. The other kids followed her lead.

"I found the windows!" said Georgie, pulling the heavy fabric back to expose a corner of the glass.

"It's still dark outside," said Andrea.

"At this time of day, it should be," Jack reminded her. "The storm seems to be letting up, though."

"Here's the door!" announced Josh.

It led to the entrance hall.

"Back where we started," said Jack.

"What's in here?" asked Marty, turning the knob on the door next to the screening room. She pushed it open and stepped inside. A shiny black grand piano took up half the room. Chairs, stools, music stands and a rolltop desk filled the rest.

"It's her music room," said Scott, going to the piano. "I bet she wrote her songs in here."

He sat down and ran his fingers lightly across the keys.

"Can you play?" asked Jack.

"A little," said Scott.

"Play something, Scotty," urged Andrea.

Scott looked at Jack, who nodded. "I don't see what it could hurt."

Scott thought for a minute, then began to play. *A little,* thought Marty. Scott was good. She knew he didn't have a piano at home, and wondered where he had learned to play like that.

"Do you take lessons?" she asked him when he finished.

He shook his head. "I just mess around."

"If you play that well just messing around," said Jack, "I can imagine how good you'd be if you took lessons!"

"You'd be rich and famous!" agreed Michael.

"And live in a place like this," said Brooke.

"You could buy Crestlawn!" Andrea told him. "And Mom and I could come live with you!"

Scott laughed.

"Wouldn't it be great to live here?" asked Georgie.

Marty pushed the toe of her boot into the thick carpet. "I wonder why she left."

"She was never here," said Jack. "She spent so much time in Nashville that she decided to move there."

"I bet it made her sad to give up Crestlawn," said Georgie.

"I think it did," said Jack, "but that's the other side of talent. It's not worth having unless you use it. And being rich doesn't always mean you can have everything you want."

"I'm going to be rich," announced Brooke. "I'm going to be a great dancer. That's my gift."

"You're supposed to use your gift for other people," Michael reminded her, "not to make yourself rich."

"Why can't you do both?" she asked.

"I don't think there's anything wrong with having money," said Jack. "The important thing is what you do with it."

"Like helping people," said Josh, "instead of spending it on bowling alleys and swimming pools!"

"She helps people, too," said Marty. "She gives money to the hospital all the time."

"I didn't know that," said Megan.

"I hope I can help people with my gift," Marty sighed, "if I can ever find out what it is."

"You'll find it," said Jack, "in God's time. Remember?"

Marty nodded.

After a long pause, Jack said, "I feel like singing. Play something for us, Scott."

"OK," said Scott, and launched into "What a Friend We Have in Jesus."

Gathered around the piano, they sang warm, happy songs until the wind stopped hurling snow against the windows. Marty looked outside. Moonlight had found a break in the clouds and spilled across snow-covered fields. The storm was over.

Jack went back through the house to make sure all the lights were off. Marty and the others waited for him in the entrance hall. They sat on the marble steps of the wide, curved staircase.

"We didn't get to see upstairs," complained Andrea.

"It's probably just bedrooms," said Scott.

"But Crestlawn bedrooms," Brooke reminded him.

When Jack returned, Marty stood to put on her coat. "Are you sure it's safe to go home now?" she asked him.

"They've probably got the snowplows out to clear the streets," he said. "We'll be fine in the van."

"Tomorrow's Saturday," said Georgie hopefully. "We could spend the night, if we had to."

Jack laughed. "Sorry guys, the adventure's over. Everybody into the van!"

As Marty waded through snow drifts a foot deep on the portico, Andrea tiptoed behind her, carefully placing her feet in Marty's tracks.

"I hate snow!" she grumbled.

Chapter Eight

Marty loved snow. She liked the way it blanketed everything and made the world look fresh and new. As she rode with her family to church, she watched the Sunday morning sunshine sparkle on the crisp, white surface until her eyes ached.

"If you don't stop that," said Jack, "you'll get snow blindness."

"What's that?"

"You won't be able to see."

"Snow can't make you blind," said Marty, but she didn't know whether he was teasing or not. "Can it, Mom?"

"It can when the sun is bright like this," she said. "It creates a glare that can hurt your eyes, if you stare at it long enough."

"Then it's the sun that does it," Marty argued, "and not the snow."

"It's the sun *and* the snow," said Jack.

When they got to church, Marty and her mom walked slowly on the snow-covered walk into the building. Once inside, Marty's mom gave her hand a gentle squeeze.

"Wait a minute," she whispered.

Puzzled, Marty waited. She watched her dad and Jack join a group of men at the other side of the narthex. Finally, her mom turned to her, smiling.

"What did you say to your brother Friday night?"

"About what?"

"About church. He said you two had a talk while you were stranded at Crestlawn."

"I don't know," Marty said slowly, trying to remember.

"Well, whatever it was, you're the reason he decided to come this morning."

"Really?"

"That's what he said." Her mom hugged her. "We'd better go. We'll be late for Sunday school."

Marty remembered asking Jack if he was glad he went to church Wednesday night. She was only trying to understand what Mrs. Cole had told her, but if it made him decide to come back, that was OK, too.

During fellowship time, between Sunday school and morning worship, Marty found herself alone with Pastor Hollis at the doughnut table.

"May I ask you something?" Marty looked into the pastor's eyes.

"You may ask me anything," he told her. "What's it about?"

"Spiritual gifts."

Pastor Hollis pretended to be surprised. "You've been listening to my sermons!"

Marty grinned.

"What about spiritual gifts?" he asked.

"The Bible says I have one, right?"

"Right. All believers are given gifts of the Spirit."

"Then how can I find out what mine is?"

Pastor Hollis took a bite of doughnut and thought. "Well, let's see . . . The first step is to pray. Have you done that?"

Marty shook her head.

"Who gives you your gift?"

"The Holy Spirit."

"Right. So you need to ask Him to guide you, and you need to promise that when you find it, you'll use it for God. Can you do that?"

"Yes."

"Good. After that, I guess you could start with the things you do well."

"But there isn't anything. I've tried writing and drawing and singing . . ."

"I think you're confusing spiritual gifts with creative ability."

"You mean they're different?"

"Creative ability is only one of the spiritual gifts. There are lots of others."

"Oh."

"I'll tell you what. See me after morning worship and I'll give you some Scripture references to look up. OK?"

"OK. Thanks, Pastor Hollis!"

That afternoon, when Georgie came over, Marty was in her room reading the Bible.

"Look," said Marty, handing her the list she had been making.

"Service, teaching, giving, leadership . . ." read Georgie. "What's this?"

"Spiritual gifts."

"Wow! I didn't know there were so many."

"Pastor Hollis says there's more, too. He says creative ability is only one of them."

"Maybe that's why we can't find yours."

"Jack says I'm creative in a different way."

"That's what I meant," said Georgie quickly.

Marty grinned. "I know."

"There's a whole bunch of stuff you haven't tried yet." Georgie looked at the list again and frowned. "What's 'tongues'?"

"I don't know," admitted Marty. "I haven't figured that one out yet."

"Here's healing. That's what your mom does."

"Would hers be healing or mercy? Or helping others?"

"Maybe a nurse has all three."

Marty nodded. "I think Dad's is administration. Doesn't that mean being the boss?"

"I think so. Which one do you think is yours?"

"I don't know. What do you think?"

Georgie shrugged, then her face lit up. "I know! You could hang out with your mom and see if you like nursing."

"Or I could go to the office with my dad," said Marty.

"You could try both."

"I wonder if Jack would teach me how to fly an airplane."

Georgie giggled.

The following Friday, Marty's mom picked her up after school and took her to work with her. Marty had been to the hospital plenty of times before. Usually, though, she went to the children's ward and read to the toddlers, or helped some of the younger kids with their school work. This time, she stayed with her mom.

Marty liked checking on the patients. She wished she could spend more time with them, but just as she was getting to know someone, her mom was ready to move on. Marty didn't mind the needles or the blood, or the messes that people made when they weren't feeling well. What she didn't like was the long names everything had.

"You'd get used to that," said her mom. "After all the biology and chemistry courses you'd have to take, those big words wouldn't bother you anymore."

"Biology and chemistry?"

"To be a nurse, you have to learn everything you can about the human body."

"Oh."

Marty didn't like the sound of that. She made good grades in science, but mostly her classes were about nature—plants and animals, and how they got along with each other. She didn't think studying the insides of things would be nearly as interesting.

After supper in the hospital cafeteria, Marty asked her mom if she could go to the children's ward. "They'll be trying to get the little kids to sleep and I could help read to them."

"Are you tired of nursing already?"

Marty grinned. "I guess so. It would be more fun to sit down and talk to the patients for a while."

"I think so, too," said her mom, "but a nurse doesn't have time to do much of that."

"I know."

"Do you know what I think? I think you're a people person. Why don't you ask your dad about his job? He talks to people all day long."

"I was going to. Do you think he'd let me go with him and Jack to the office tomorrow?"

"Jack has to go to the city, but I think your dad would love it."

On Saturday, Marty went to work with her dad. He showed her around the office. His secretary, Mrs. Bailey, taught her how to use all the equipment. She liked the computer best. By following the instructions in a manual, she drew a picture of a house.

"That's very good, Marty," said Mrs. Bailey. "It took me a week to figure out how to do that!"

Marty grinned. "Thanks."

"Your dad says you're looking for your talent. Maybe it's computers."

"Maybe."

She had learned some computer programming at school, though, and wasn't very good at it. When the instructions were already written down, she could follow them. When she had to make it up, she couldn't do it.

For lunch, Marty's dad took her to a sandwich shop down the street from his office.

"Are you having a good time?" he asked her.

"Yes, but I thought I'd be helping you, not Mrs. Bailey."

"But I don't do anything you could help with."

"What do you do?"

"Mostly I talk to people."

"Couldn't I listen? I wouldn't say anything."

Her dad gave her a thoughtful look. "Are you really interested in all this?"

"I don't know yet."

He laughed. "Fair enough."

After lunch, he let her sit in his office while he talked with clients. She didn't understand most of what was said.

"There are clients who want to sell and clients who want to buy," he explained. "It's my job to put the right buyer with the right seller so everybody gets what they want."

It sounded easy, but looked hard. There were all kinds of papers to fill out, and there was a lot of math. Marty wasn't very good at math.

On the way home that afternoon, her dad asked, "Well, what do you think about the real estate business?"

"I think it's hard."

Her dad laughed.

"Jack says you're good at it," she told him.

"Jack's good at it, too," he said. "That's why I can't let him throw it away."

Chapter Nine

"This isn't working," said Marty.

"What isn't?" asked Andrea, handing her and Georgie sodas from the refrigerator.

"Finding spiritual gifts is harder than finding talents!"

Marty and Georgie were spending Sunday afternoon at Andrea's. Andrea had her magazines from the sixties spread out on the kitchen table and they were helping her find pictures about the civil rights movement.

"You can't give up," said Georgie.

"I'm not giving up," said Marty. "I just don't think I'm doing it right."

"Maybe you're doing it backwards," suggested Scott from the doorway, sipping an orange soda.

"What do you mean?" asked Marty.

"You've been trying different things to see if you're good at them," he explained, walking over to the table. "Maybe you should think of what you're good at and see if it's a spiritual gift."

Marty sighed. "I tried that first, but I couldn't think of anything."

"There has to be something, right? The Bible says so."

"I guess so."

Scott pulled out a chair and sat down. "We'll help you figure it out. What do you think she's good at, Georgie?"

"Taking tests," said Georgie. "She always makes good grades and she never gets nervous."

"That's because I study," said Marty. "Tests are no big deal if you study for them."

"I study, too," said Andrea, "but then they ask questions that I didn't study for!"

"That's what I mean," said Georgie. "Marty always knows what to study. How do you do that?"

Marty shrugged. "I don't know. I just study from the notes I take in class."

"Maybe that's what she's good at," suggested Andrea, "taking notes."

"She's good at explaining things, too," said Georgie.

"That's right!" agreed Andrea. "Marty explains things better than the teacher does sometimes."

"Did anyone ever tell you that you'd make a good teacher?" Scott asked Marty.

"Mrs. Cole, at church," said Marty. "She lets me help her with the little kids."

"And teaching's one of the spiritual gifts!" said Georgie.

Scott stood up and pushed his chair back under the table. "There you go," he said, and left the room.

"*That* was easy," said Marty.

After church that night, as Marty shook hands

with Pastor Hollis, he asked, "How's the search coming, Marty? Has the Spirit led you to your gift yet?"

"I think so," she told him.

"Good! What do you think it is?"

"I think it's teaching."

As soon as she said the word, Marty knew she was right.

"I found it," she announced to her family as they drove home from church.

"Found what, honey?" asked her mom.

"I found my gift. It's teaching."

"That's great, T.J." said Jack.

Her mom smiled at her. "I think you'll make a wonderful teacher."

"She taught Mrs. Bailey how to use the computer!" said her dad.

Marty giggled. "No, I didn't."

"As long as we're making announcements," said Jack, "I have one, too. I got a job."

Marty looked at her dad, but he stared straight ahead and didn't say anything.

"A big corporation in the city wants to train me to fly one of their company jets," Jack continued. "I signed the contract yesterday."

Marty grinned at Jack and he winked at her, but no one said anything else until they got home. Then her mom said, "Go get ready for bed, Marty."

Marty knew her dad was angry. She knew her mom had sent her to her room so he could talk to Jack. But her room was next to the den, and when her dad was angry, she could hear his voice through the wall.

"I thought we had this settled," he said.

"I told you I'd stay until I found a job as a pilot," said Jack. "But you didn't think I'd find one. That's the only reason you agreed to it."

"I need you, Jack."

"No, you don't. If business was bad, maybe, but business is great."

"That's all the more reason I need your help."

"You need help, but it doesn't have to be me. I'm sorry, Dad. You're going to have to hire somebody else."

"I don't want somebody else!"

There was a long pause, and Marty's breathing suddenly sounded very loud in her ears. When Jack finally spoke, his voice was softer.

"You said you wanted me to be happy. Flying makes me happy."

"But is it something you can count on?" asked her dad.

"I think so, because I'm good at it."

"You're good at selling real estate, too."

"But selling real estate is what makes *you* happy, Dad, not me."

"It used to make me happy, when I was building up the business for you!"

"I'm sorry," said Jack.

"I'm sorry, too, Son. That wasn't fair and it wasn't true. My work does make me happy. I've just been too busy lately to enjoy it."

"You're tired. You've got to hire someone to help you."

"I know, but finding the right person isn't easy."

"Would you like a suggestion?" asked Jack.

"Don't say Marty," teased her dad. "She's decided real estate isn't for her, either!"

Marty grinned as she heard Jack laugh from the other side of the wall.

"I was going to recommend Judy Bailey," said Jack.

"My secretary?"

"She knows more about the business than you do!"

"I know, but what makes you think she wants to be an agent?"

"She told me."

"Why didn't she tell me?"

"I guess you never asked."

"I guess I didn't. OK, I'll talk to her tomorrow."

In her room, Marty smiled. She felt the way she had when she looked out the window at Crestlawn and saw that the storm was over. *Thank you, God,* she prayed. *And thanks for leading me to my spiritual gift.*

Marty finished her homework and was about to turn out the light when she heard a soft knock at the door.

"Come in," she called.

Jack opened the door. "I just wanted to say good night."

"'Night. Jack?"

"Yes?"

"Are you going to be moving away now?"

"Why? Are you going to take over my room?"

"I'm serious."

Jack walked over and sat on the side of her bed. "Yes, T.J., I'll be moving, but not for a couple of months, at least. After the training period is over and I'm sure they want me as a pilot, I'll find a place of my own."

"Couldn't you just stay here?"

"I could, but it's time for me to move out. You'll feel the same way when you're my age. Besides, I won't be far away. I'll see you more often than I did when I was at college."

"Will you still go to our church?"

Jack grinned. "Is that what this is about?"

"What?"

"You're sneaky, young lady! But you're right. I do need to go to church. I know that. And, thanks to you, I also know that I *want* to go to church. So you can stop worrying, OK?"

Marty frowned. "I just thought if you went to our church, I'd see you every week."

Jack looked closely at her face, then shook his head slowly. "You really are a teacher, Marty J. You taught me a lesson and you didn't even know it."

"I did?"

"Yes, you did. See? I told you you'd find something you're good at."

"I like it, too," said Marty, "but it doesn't help me very much with my Black History Month project."

"What's that?"

"It's supposed to be something special about black history. I thought when I found my gift, I'd know what to do for my project. But that's when I thought it was going to be something creative."

"Teaching can be creative," said Jack. "You'll think of something."

"That's what everybody keeps saying," complained Marty, "but what if I don't?"

"You will. You like history. It's one of your favorite subjects."

"I know, but . . ."

"But, nothing. Think like a teacher, T.J.! Start

with the subject. What part of black history do you want to cover?"

"I don't know."

"Well, decide! Then, when you know *what* you want to talk about, start thinking about how you want to say it."

"That's the hard part."

"Not for a teacher. Think about your teachers at school. How do they make things interesting? Who were the best history teachers you ever had? What did they do? Why did you like them? Do you see what I mean?"

Marty nodded. She really did understand.

Jack grinned and hugged her. "You'll think of something special," he told her. "You've got a gift, remember?"

Chapter Ten

Think like a teacher, T.J.!

Marty spent the next week in the library. Every time she had a few spare minutes, she'd ask her teacher, Miss Morris, for a library pass.

"I can't wait to see your project," said Miss Morris.

Marty smiled. *Me neither,* she thought.

"You've been working so hard," said Miss Morris. "I just know it's going to be special."

I hope so, thought Marty. The truth was, she still didn't know what she was going to do. But Jack had given her a way to find out.

Think like a teacher, T.J.!

Marty looked at everything listed in the black history section of the card catalog. She read about leaders from Ralph Abernathy to Andrew Young. She learned of bus boycotts and freedom marches. She studied black artists and their music, plays, paintings, and sculptures.

Marty found so much interesting material that she almost gave up hope of ever being able to pick just one topic to cover. Then she noticed something, The more she read, the more she found one name showing up over and over. All the leaders talked about him. Artists celebrated his life. The name was Dr. Martin Luther King, Jr.

Marty decided to make Dr. King the subject of her project. Andrea had already suggested it. And she was right. Marty did know a lot about him, and she was learning more every day. She took out her notes and put stars by the sections about Dr. King. There was plenty of material.

The next step was to figure out how to present it.

Think like a teacher, T.J.!

On Saturday, Marty asked all the Grace Street Kids to come over. They met in the den and her mom popped popcorn for them.

"Great party," said Josh. "What's it for?"

"I want to ask you some questions," said Marty.

"What kind of questions?" asked Megan.

"Like, who was the best teacher you ever had?"

Josh grinned. "Is this a joke?"

"No," said Marty. "It's for my project."

"Your project?" asked Georgie. "What are you going to do?"

"You thought of something and didn't tell us!" said Andrea.

"I'm telling you now," said Marty, "and I didn't really think of anything, yet. That's why I need your help."

"I don't understand," said Brooke.

"She wants to brainstorm!" said Scott.

"I don't think I've ever done that," Brooke said.

"You have to have a brain, first," Michael told her.

"It just means we all sit around and talk about it," said Scott, "until somebody gets an idea."

"OK," agreed Josh. "What do we talk about?"

"Teachers," said Marty. "I'm going to do my project on Martin Luther King . . ."

"That was my idea!" said Andrea with pride.

"But I don't know how to do it, yet," Marty finished.

"What's that got to do with teachers?" asked Josh.

"You'll see," said Marty. "Who was your favorite teacher?"

"Mr. Kimsey," said Josh.

"He teaches P.E.," said Michael.

"Nobody said it couldn't be a P.E. teacher," said Josh.

"My favorite was Mrs. Leatherby," said Megan.

Josh made a face.

"I liked her," insisted Megan.

"Why?" asked Marty.

Megan shrugged. "I don't know. She's really nice, and she made things interesting."

"That's what I need to know," said Marty. "How did she do that?"

"Oh—OK! Let's see. One time she brought a snake to class when we were studying reptiles."

"Mr. Prescott took us to a pond," said Michael.

"He took us, too," said Marty. "Field trips are great, but I need something that will help me with my project."

"Maybe you could do a pretend field trip," suggested Georgie.

"What do you mean?"

"You could show pictures of important places in Dr. King's life."

"Or slides," said Andrea.

"Or home videos!" said Brooke.

"Sounds great," said Marty, "but where would I get them?"

Nobody had an answer.

"You know what I like?" said Georgie. "I like when Mr. Prescott lets us work by ourselves."

"Learning centers!" said Marty. "Georgie, that's a great idea!"

"You can get video tapes of Dr. King's speeches at the library," suggested Scott.

Marty grabbed her notebook and started a list. "Can I go through your magazines?" she asked Andrea. "There may be some articles about him."

"Sure," said Andrea. "I only need the pictures."

"I found dozens of quotes about him from the people who knew him," said Marty. "There ought to be some way I can use those."

"How about baseball cards?" asked Josh.

Everybody laughed.

"I'm totally serious," said Josh.

"About baseball cards?" asked Megan.

"Well, not actual baseball cards," he said, "but something like that. You could put their pictures on the front and what they said about Dr. King on the back."

"That's good, Josh," said Scott. "Andrea can share her pictures."

Andrea glared at him.

"You don't need *all* of them," he told her.

"I'll just use the ones you don't want for your

collage," said Marty. "Will you help me pick out some good ones?"

Andrea brightened. "OK."

"And I can tell who they were and how they knew Dr. King," said Marty. "This is great. Thanks, everybody."

"Hey, no problem," said Josh.

At church on Sunday, Mrs. Cole asked Marty to become her official assistant group leader for children on Wednesday nights.

"Pastor Hollis says you have a teaching gift, and I confirm it," she told Marty. Then she added with a wink, "That means I think you have a teaching gift, too."

"But I already help you with the little kids," said Marty.

"I know, but this would be different. You'd have to help me every week, and sometimes you'd have to be with the children instead of doing things with the kids your own age. Would you want to do that?"

"Sure."

"Good. Then it's official."

Marty grinned. She liked the sound of that.

"I'll tell you something about spiritual gifts," said Mrs. Cole. "The church has a responsibility to help its members develop them."

"It does?"

"Yes, and you're very lucky that you already know what yours is."

"I know. It's only teaching, but at least there's *something* I'm good at."

"What do you mean, 'it's *only* teaching'?"

"Well, it's not creative, like dancing or writing."

"Marty Wilson, I'm ashamed of you!"

Marty was speechless with surprise at Mrs. Cole's words.

"Pastor Hollis told me you'd been reading about spiritual gifts," she said.

Marty nodded.

"Well, you'd better get your Bible out and read it again if you think teaching isn't as good as creative ability!"

"I just meant . . ."

"Don't you know that teaching is one of the highest ranked gifts in the Bible?"

"It is?"

"It certainly is. Now that doesn't mean you're any *better* than anybody else because you have that gift. All the gifts are important, because they all come from the Spirit. But teaching gifts are necessary for the church to grow. It's a very special responsibility. Do you understand?"

"I think so."

Mrs. Cole smiled. "I hope you do, Marty. You're a very special person and you're talented."

Marty frowned and Mrs. Cole laughed.

"You're a talented teacher," she explained. "You have to stop thinking of all talent as creative ability."

"OK," said Marty with a grin, "and I'm sorry I thought teachers weren't important."

"You should be! Just think about it, Marty. One person with creative ability can reach a lot of people in a lifetime. But one *teacher* can reach all those people, and give *each one* the knowledge to reach that many more! And if just *one* of them becomes a teacher . . . it's endless!"

Marty tried to think about is, but it was like the branches of the Owl Tree. There were hundreds. Maybe thousands! There was only one thing she was sure of: she couldn't *wait* to get started on her Black History Month project!